WILI WAI KULA
and the
THREE MONGOOSES

By Donivee Martin Laird
Illustrated by Carol Jossem

Barnaby Books Honolulu, Hawaii

Also by Barnaby Books
The Three Little Hawaiian Pigs and the Magic Shark
(The Three Little Pigs)
Keaka and the Liliko'i Vine
(Jack and the Beanstalk)
'Ula Li'i and the Magic Shark
(Little Red Riding Hood)

Published by:
Barnaby Books - a Hawaii partnership
3290 Pacific Heights Road
Honolulu, Hawaii 96813

Printed and bound in Hong Kong under the direction of:
Printing Force Company

Library of Congress Catalog Number 83-8805

ISBN 0-940350-24-6

Fifth printing 6/94

TO THE SCHOOL CHILDREN OF HAWAII WHO ARE OUR FAITHFUL CRITICS AND FRIENDS.

PRONUNCIATION GUIDE

The 12 letters in the Hawaiian alphabet are:
A, E, H, I, K, L, M, N, O, P, U, W

consonants
H, K, L, M, N, P are pronounced as in English
W is usually pronounced as V

vowels
A like a in farm
E like e in set
I like y in pretty

O like o in hold
U like oo in soon

plural
As there is no S in Hawaiian, the plural is formed by word usage or the addition of another word such as nā to the sentence.

THE LANGUAGE SPOKEN BY THE MONGOOSES IS PIDGIN ENGLISH. IN USING THIS DIALECT. THE AUTHOR HAS NO WISH TO OFFEND ANYONE, BUT ONLY TO SHARE THE SPECIAL FLAVOR PIDGIN ENGLISH ADDS TO HAWAII.

Once upon a time, deep in a Hawaiian forest, there lived a family of three mongooses.

There was Papa Mongoose who spoke with a deep, gruff voice, Mama Mongoose who spoke with a soft, sweet voice and Baby Mongoose who spoke with a high, squeaky voice.

One morning, Mama Mongoose fixed rice and Portuguese sausage for breakfast. When the meal was ready, it was too hot to eat. Papa Mongoose suggested taking a walk and leaving the food on the table to cool. Away the family went, happily strolling down the path.

At that very same time, Wili Wai Kula, a little girl with curly golden hair, set off on her morning walk. She was a cheerful child who was full of high spirits. She had a great deal of curiosity and a habit of doing the very thing she was told not to do.

This sunny morning was no different. As Wili Wai Kula left home her mother said, "Now Wili, don't you forget that you are still too young to go into the forest alone."

"Yes mother," answered Wili Wai Kula with a grin.

Of course, just as soon as she was out of her mother's sight, the forest is precisely where Wili Wai Kula went.

"I'll go only a little way. Just to see what it is like," she told herself as she walked along. On and on she went, listening to the birds and admiring the kukui trees. Finally, she was deep, deep in the forest. Then, just when she was about to turn back, she saw the little mongoose house tucked between two large, leafy mango trees.

"Oh, what a cute little hale!" exclaimed Wili Wai Kula, "I wonder who lives here." She tiptoed up to the window and peeked inside. No one was in sight.

She knocked softly at the door. No one answered. She pushed the door gently. When it swung open, she stepped into the house and looked around.

"Is anyone here?" She called in a shaky voice. There was no answer. She felt braver and walked further into the room. The first thing she saw was the table and its three plates of rice and Portuguese sausage.

"Oh! The mea'ai smells so 'ono," said a hungry Wili Wai Kula.
She tasted the rice and sausage on the biggest plate. It was too hot. Next,
she tasted the rice and sausage on the medium-sized plate. It was too cold.

But the littlest plate, ah, the littlest plate was just right. So, without thinking twice about whose breakfast she might be eating, Wili Wai Kula ate every bit. When she was pau, she drank all the guava juice from the blue cup beside the littlest plate.

On the other side of the room there were three koa rocking chairs. Wili Wai Kula's 'ōpū was full. She felt content. The chairs looked comfortable and seemed to invite her to sit and rock.

She climbed up and sat in the biggest chair. It was too wide. Next, she tried the medium-sized chair. It was too narrow.

But the littlest chair, ah, the littlest chair was just right. So she sat back and relaxed.

Suddenly, with a loud crack, the chair fell apart. Wili Wai Kula tumbled on to the floor with a painful thump.

Standing up slowly and rubbing her sore 'elemu, Wili Wai Kula noticed a staircase leading to the second floor.

"I wonder what is up those stairs?" she thought. Full of curiosity, she tried standing on her toes, but she could see nothing. Then she stood on the bottom step, stretching her neck as far as she could.

She still couldn't see. "I can't leave here without seeing what is up there," she whispered as slowly she went up, one step at a time. Goodness how she hoped she wouldn't meet anyone at the top.

To her relief, no one was around. All she found was a bedroom with three pūne'e in it. The pūne'e looked warm and cosy and Wili Wai Kula was tired.

She tried the biggest pūneʻe. It was too hard. Next, she tried the medium-sized pūneʻe. It was too soft.

But the littlest pūneʻe, ah, the littlest pūneʻe was just right. So, Wili Wai Kula climbed under the blue and white quilt, yawned, and in a blink was sound asleep.

Out on the forest path, the mongooses were returning from their walk. They were hungry and anxious for their breakfast.

When they were seated at the table, Papa Mongoose looked at his food suspiciously. "Ey! Somebody wen eat my rice and Portagee sausage," he said in his deep, gruff voice.

Then Mama Mongoose said, in her soft, sweet voice, "Somebody wen eat my rice and Portagee sausage."

And Baby Mongoose said, in his high squeaky voice, "Somebody wen eat my rice and Portagee sausage. And da bugga wen eat 'em all up." His lips began to tremble.

Papa and Mama Mongoose shared their breakfast with Baby Mongoose. When everyone had had enough to eat, they turned their attention to the mystery of the missing food. They went to sit in their rocking chairs where they could talk things over in comfort.

"Ey! Somebody wen seet on top my rock-a," said Papa Mongoose in his deep, gruff voice.

Then Mama Mongoose said, in her soft, sweet voice, "Somebody wen seet on top my rock-a."

And Baby Mongoose said, in his high, squeaky voice, "Somebody wen seet on top my rock-a and da bugga wen bus 'em all up." And he began to cry.

Papa Mongoose dried his tears and Mama Mongoose assured him that she could fix his chair. Quietly and carefully they went upstairs together to check on the rest of their house.

"Ey! Somebody wen sleep inside my pūne'e," said Papa Mongoose in his deep, gruff voice.

Then Mama Mongoose said, in her soft, sweet voice, "Somebody wen sleep inside my pūne'e."

"How you like dat nerve?" shrieked Baby Mongoose in his highest, squeakiest voice. "One wahine stay sleeping inside my pūne'e. And she stay stop yet."

Baby Mongoose's high, squeaky voice woke Wili Wai Kula. She opened her eyes and saw three mongooses with angry faces and sharp teeth.

Giving a frightened yell, she leaped off the pūneʻe.

Down the stairs she tumbled.

Out
the door
she
crashed.

Through the forest she ran.

Up her front steps she jumped
and into her own house she
dashed. She didn't stop until
she was safe inside with
the door locked behind her.
To her mother's surprise,
she didn't go out again for three
whole days.

After that morning walk, Wili Wai Kula was much better about minding her mother and father. She continued to be full of curiosity and high spirits and she still got into mischief. And when she did her family shook their heads saying, "At least she stays out of the forest."

There was another lesson Wili Wai Kula learned. That lesson was . . . Never, never go into a mongoose's house without first being invited.

GLOSSARY

WILI WAI KULA Wili used here means twisting lock of hair. Wai Kula means gold-colored. Together they say Goldilocks.

MONGOOSE A slender animal with a pointed face, long tail, and smooth brown fur. A member of the viverrine family.

PORTUGUESE SAUSAGE A linguisa or spicy sausage, popular in Hawaii.

KUKUI TREE The candlenut tree, a large tree common in Hawaiian forests. Nuts from this tree are black and when polished are strung into leis. The very oily nut meats were once used as lamps and lamp oil. The meat is also roasted and used as a relish.

MANGO A tropical fruit, eaten raw or cooked and used in chutneys and mango bread. Fruit is fairly large and has juicy yellow meat and one large seed.

HALE Hawaiian word for house.

'ONO Meaning good, delicious, or tasty in Hawaiian.

PAU   A Hawaiian word for finished, ended, completed.

MEA'AI   A Hawaiian word for food.

'ŌPŪ   Hawaiian word meaning stomach.

'ĒLEMU   The Hawaiian way of saying buttocks.

KOA   Member of the acacia family and largest of Hawaii's forest trees. The wood is used for furniture, canoes, and other kinds of woodwork.

PŪNE'E   A flat couch, usually without arms or backrest, used as a bed.

WAHINE   Hawaiian word for woman.

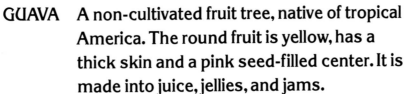

GUAVA   A non-cultivated fruit tree, native of tropical America. The round fruit is yellow, has a thick skin and a pink seed-filled center. It is made into juice, jellies, and jams.